Tudor Tales

The Thief, the Fool and the Big Fat King

Terry Deary

Illustrated by Helen Flook

*This book is dedicated to the memory
of the hundreds of people who died for
the greed and stupidity of the monstrous
King Henry VIII – Terry Deary*

First published 2003 by
A & C Black Publishers Ltd
37 Soho Square, London W1D 3QZ
www.acblack.com

Text copyright © 2003 Terry Deary
Illustrations copyright © 2003 Helen Flook

The rights of Terry Deary and Helen Flook to be identified
as the author and illustrator of this work respectively have been
asserted by them in accordance with the Copyrights, Designs
and Patents Act 1988.

ISBN 0-7136-6434-7

A CIP catalogue for this book is available from the
British Library.

A & C Black uses paper produced with elemental
chlorine-free pulp, harvested from managed sustainable forests.

Printed and bound in Spain by G. Z. Printek, Bilbao.

1 Cowards and coffins

'Lay-deez and gennle-men!' my father cried to the crowd that gathered round. 'See this poor, hungry little boy?' he roared, pointing at me.

People drifted from every corner of the churchyard to see what was going on. There must have been five hundred people in St Paul's churchyard that day: meeting friends, doing business or just watching the entertainers. Entertainers like me and my father. He kicked me on the ankle.

'Oh!' I cried. 'Oh! Oh! Oh! I am so-o-o hungry! I would do anything for a crust of bread!'

The truth was, I was full of mutton pie, but you have to put on an act if you want to make some money.

About fifty people pushed and jostled to get a better view. My father lifted me on to the rough wooden coffin we had brought with us.

'This little boy is so-o-o hungry he is willing to risk his life to make a few pennies.'

'What's he going to do?' a tangle-haired girl called out. 'Jump off the coffin?'

The crowd laughed. Father turned red. 'He is going to let me stab him!' my father shouted and the laughter died suddenly.

'Tshah!' the girl sneered. 'I'll give you a penny if you let me do it.' She pulled a knife from the pocket of her scruffy brown dress and waved it under my nose. 'I'll cut his head clean off.'

My father tried to ignore her. He pulled off his green cap and held it out. 'Come on, lay-deez and gennle-men! Give just a few pennies to see this terrible sight!'

'Oh!' I cried. 'Oh! Oh! Oh! I am so-o-o hungry! I would do anything for a crust of bread!'

A thin man in a yellow jerkin and red trousers shouted, 'Let's see you stab him first!'

The rest of the crowd agreed. 'Stab him first!'

And the tangle-haired girl said, 'Let me do it!'

My father slapped his cap back on. 'Oh, very well,' he snapped. 'I will stab him.' He turned to me. 'Are you ready, my dear little, darling little boy?'

I squeezed my eyes tight shut and squeaked, 'Yes, my dear father. But if I die please give my love to Mummy!'

The crowd shuffled and sniffed and looked unsure now. Even the tangle-haired girl in the scruffy brown dress was watching in silence.

'If I get it wrong and I kill you, will you forgive me, little James?'

'I forgive you, Father,' I sighed.

I wished he'd get on with it. But I knew he was waiting till everyone in the graveyard was watching. The bigger the audience, the more money we'd make.

'Lay-deez and gennle-men,' Father went on and I opened my eyes a little. 'This is no trick. See this knife is sharp enough to shave a swine!'

He reached forward, grabbed the girl in the brown dress and sliced off a lump of her tangled hair with a stroke.

The crowd gasped.

'Oi! What you doing?' the girl raged and her face, under the dirty smudges, glowed red with anger. I tried not to laugh.

My father turned to me. He raised the knife high into the air so the spring sunlight glittered on the blade. It was so quiet I'll swear you could hear the worms below the graveyard chewing away at the bodies.

The knife swept down and struck me in the stomach.

2 Blood and bladders

'Oh, Father!' I gasped and clutched at my stomach. The cold blood trickled through my fingers. The crowd shouted and cried in confusion.

'Oh, dear Father, I think you have killed me!'

I moved to the end of the coffin and fell into his arms.

'My son, my James, my little Jimmy!' he wept. 'I have your coffin here,' he said.

I let myself go limp in his arms. He kicked open the lid and lowered me into the box.

The lid slammed and I was in darkness.

That didn't matter. I'd done this fifty times before, all over England and Wales. I didn't need light. I wriggled out of the blood-wet shirt and untied the pig's stomach that was strapped to my waist.

There was still some pig's blood in it and I wrapped it quickly in the shirt and stuffed it in the hidden cubbyhole at the head of the coffin.

I took off the wooden board that was strapped to my belly – the one that had stopped the knife really going into me.

I placed it, clean side out, over the secret cubbyhole so the blood-stained shirt was hidden. The board fitted perfectly – it was made to.

No one who looked in the coffin would find the shirt. I groped at my feet and found

a clean shirt and struggled into it. I could hear muffled voices through the thin wood.

Father was crying, 'Is there no one who can help me in my hour of despair? I cannot even afford to bury my little James!'

Then I heard a woman's voice say, 'I have heard of a spell that will raise the dead – if you say it quickly enough. And it will only work the once!'

I heard the crowd gasp and shuffle away.
I heard them mutter in terror 'Witchcraft!',
and you could be hanged for witchcraft.

'Please say the words, good woman!'
Father groaned.

'Sorry, dear sir,' she sighed. 'I need
silver and gold in my hands or the spell
will never work – and I am a poor woman!'

'Has no one any silver or gold?' Father
cried.

There was a chinking and tinkling as the
the crowd opened their purses and
placed the money in the
woman's hands.

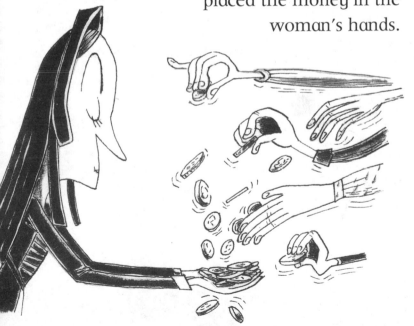

I heard the woman place her hands on the top of the coffin. I heard her rest her head on the coffin lid ...

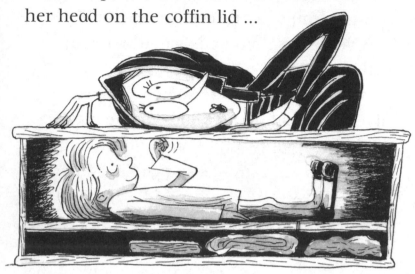

... and mutter the strange Egyptian words she had learned.

Ofano, Oblamo, Ospergo.
Pax Sax Sarax.
Afa Afca Nostra.
Cerum Heaium Lada Frium!

Then the coffin lid was thrown open and the woman looked in. No one could see me as I gave her a quick grin and mouthed, 'Hello, Mum!'

3 Catpurses and confusion

My mother called, 'Rise from your coffin, child.'

I blinked.
I sat up.

I struggled to my feet and felt my stomach. The crowd gasped. They'd seen the blood flow and they'd seen it stain my shirt. Now my shirt was as white as the April clouds above the churchyard.

Father fell to his knees and kissed Mother's hands. 'Thank you, good lady – a father's thousand thanks!'

The crowd sighed, 'Ahhhh!'
and this time, as Father
passed round the
hat, it was filled.

But no one noticed the girl with the hair as wild as a bramble bush.

'Here!' she screeched. 'It was all a trick! Here's the shirt and here's a pig's bladder full of blood. You've been robbed!'

She must have slipped round to the open coffin and opened the secret panel. Now she was holding up the blood-soaked shirt.

Suddenly an angry mob snatched at Father's hat.

He was smacked with the blade of a gentleman's sword and I was kicked with a dusty boot. We went to pick up the coffin but the crowd had already trampled it to firewood.

Then there was a new cry in the crowd. 'My purse has gone! There are cutpurses in the churchyard!'

The mob forgot about us as more people discovered they had lost their purses of silver.

We took the chance to escape from St Paul's, hurry down Fleet Street and hide in the stinking darkness of The Dead Duck tavern.

Mother flopped on to a bench and sighed. 'That cutpurse saved us a lot of trouble!'

Father shook his head angrily. 'No, the cutpurse *caused* us all the trouble! It was that girl in the brown dress. She showed the crowd how we did the swindle. She *knew* there would be trouble. It's an old cutpurse trick. While people are in a riot they forget about the purses that hung from their belts. She ran around and stole their cash.'

I nodded sadly. 'She had the knife all ready, didn't she?'

Father groaned. 'We've no money.'

'No coffin,' Mother added.

'No blood bladder,' I reminded them.

'And no bed for the night,' the fat landlord said softly. 'You already owe me for the mutton pies you had at breakfast. If you've no money you can get out now!'

We rose wearily to our sore feet and trudged to the door.

'Things can't get much worse,' Father said.

Oh, but they could!

4 A fool and a father

A man stepped out from the shadow of a doorway. He wore a yellow jerkin and red trousers; he was the man from the churchyard.

He placed a hand on my father's shoulder and Father drew his dagger fast as a butterfly's wing. 'What do you want? Money? We haven't got any. Not a penny! Go rob someone else,' Father hissed.

But the man stood in Father's way still.

'Are you a fool?' my mother asked him.

'Yes,' the man replied.

'What?' I gasped.

'Yes.'

'Yes what?'

'Yes, I'm a Fool.'

'You don't look stupid,' Mother said.

'No. I mean I am a Fool at the court of

King Henry VIII. I am Will Somers, the King's jester,' he told us eagerly.

'Are you serious?' Father asked.

'No, I'm fool-ish!' the man giggled.

We didn't laugh.

'I entertain the King with jests and songs and dancing and juggling.'

He leapt into the air …

… spun round, landed on a pile of horse droppings and slipped on his backside.

This time we laughed.

The fool didn't. He picked himself up.

'Your act in St Paul's churchyard would be perfect for the King. He loves disgusting things like that. Will you come to Hampton Court Palace with me? I have a carriage in the tavern courtyard all ready.'

'Will we be paid?' Father asked.

'With a purse of gold if the King likes you,' Will Somers said.

'Our coffin will need to be replaced,'
Father added.

'Of course.'

'Then show us to the carriage,' Father
grinned and slapped an arm round the
skinny man's yellow jerkin.

And that's how a family of
fairground cheats
came to perform
before King
Henry VIII of
England …

5 A fat king and some cards

King Henry was fat as a hog. His red face
had six chins, and greedy little eyes glinted
with the torchlight and golden chains
around his neck.

His sly-eyed queen, Anne Boleyn, watched us with a sneer.

Henry's pasty-faced daughter, Mary, trembled and prayed.

Father put on his grandest voice that night. Every time he spoke he said, 'Your Majesties, my lords, ladies and gentlemen …'

I thought he was never going to stab me! But at last the knife swept down.

I gasped, I staggered, I wailed, I fell. Princess Mary cried out.

My hands shook so much I fumbled with the board and just got it in place before my mother threw the coffin lid open.

The King roared and clapped. The rich lords sat in their velvet gowns of scarlet and gold, cornflower blue and marigold orange, and colours from every rainbow that had ever shone. When they saw Henry had enjoyed the show, they joined in with polite clapping. Anne Boleyn still sneered.

Will Somers looked pleased as he showed us down to the kitchens to eat.

A heavy purse jangled on Father's broad belt. Life was good.

'Can you play cards?' Will Somers asked.

Father looked at Mother sharply. 'A little,' he said.

'Father can make a fortune cheating at cards in the taverns,' I was going to say but Mother stepped heavily on my foot so I said, 'Father can make a for ... ouch, my foot ... sorry, Mother ... ooooh! My toes are crushed like a swatted fly!'

Will Somers said, 'The King enjoys a game of mumchance. Do you play mumchance?'

Father acted as if he didn't know. 'Er … we all name a card. Then we turn the cards one at a time. The first one to see their own card wins, is that right?'

'That's right,' came a rumbling, rich voice from the doorway. We turned to see the King limp into the kitchens.

His fat legs were covered in bandages. They say he had sores on his legs that wouldn't heal. Blood had begun to seep through the bandages and the smell was worse than The Dead Duck's mutton pies.

We bowed. The King sat heavily at a kitchen table and gave a huge belch. As Will Somers rushed to hand the King a flagon of wine, the King ordered, 'Sit down, you rogues. Give me a chance to win back some of that gold you earned tonight.'

Father sat down happily. He always won. Always.

But by the time the clock chimed midnight Father had lost every last gold piece.

6 | Cheats beats

It happened like this. Father could remember every card in the pack. He knew what cards were coming next and he named one to make sure he always won. Half-past eleven chimed ...

... and our pile of gold was growing huge.

Quarter to twelve chimed … the gold was yellow but Henry's fat face was purple with rage.

Will Somers looked on and his face was white with fear. He served Henry more wine and brought a cup for Mother and Father.

As he served Father, he whispered, 'If you want to keep your head let the King win! He hates losing!'

Father swallowed hard and scowled.
Father won the next game.

Henry was down to his last two pieces of gold. He put them in the middle of the table.

'Three of hearts,' Henry growled.

'Five of spades,' Father said quietly.

Mother turned the cards. The three of diamonds stared up at us.

'Three of hearts!' Henry cried and swept the cards off the table. He passed them back to Mother.

'It was the three of diamonds,' Father said.

Henry's bloated face grew still larger. He spoke slowly. 'Do you know what happens to a man who calls his king a liar?'

Father shook his head.

'He is taken to the Tower of London and tortured until he says he is sorry. And when he's said he is sorry he is taken to Tower Hill and hanged,' Henry explained. 'That was the three of hearts. What was it?'

Father set his jaw hard. Before he could speak, Mother cut in, 'It was the three of hearts.'

Father glared at her but stayed quiet as Henry pushed the four gold pieces back into the middle of the table. 'Again!' he ordered.

We played on. Henry cheated, Henry laughed. Henry won back all his money. He also took all the money we had earned that night.

Midnight chimed. Henry gathered the gold and staggered to his feet. 'Goodnight, Master Magician,' he snorted. 'It seems your magic let you down. Now get out of my palace, you are making it stink.'

So we found ourselves on the dark road outside the palace with a long walk back to the city and not a penny in our pockets.

Except …

When I saw the way the game was going I had walked over to Father's side and rested a hand on the table beside the gold he had left.

I wrapped a fist around one gold piece and sat back to watch. Father lost everything – but I held on to that one piece.

When the sun began to rise we were back in the city. Our feet were aching after the fifteen-mile walk. And we were starving.

'No money for food or shelter,' Father groaned. That was when I pulled out the gold piece from my pocket. He snatched it from me without a word of thanks and stalked off to The Dead Duck.

I stepped into the gloom. After the bright morning light I could hardly see. But I saw the shadow of a shadow in the far corner.

Something moved towards the back door. As the door opened, light spilled in and I could see her clearly. It was the girl in the brown dress. The cutpurse. She'd seen us enter and she was running away.

I raced across the bar-room, pushed tables and benches aside and spilled ale mugs.

I was into the stable yard at the back and saw her diving under the belly of a horse. The horseshoes sparked off the cobbles as the horse stamped and almost struck me as I dived after the girl.

As she scrambled to her feet I was there before her. I grabbed at the bag on her shoulder and it tore – spilling the purses full of coins on to the cobbles.

She looked at me, as poisonous as Henry VIII's leg.

I held tight to the remains of the bag and a couple of the purses. 'If I go to the constable with these, you'll hang.'

She shrugged. 'You don't know my name or where I live. The constable would never find me.'

At that moment the back door of the tavern opened and the fat landlord looked out, as greasy as his apron. 'What's happening, Meg?' he asked.

The girl groaned. 'Shut up, Dad!' Then she groaned again.

I nodded. 'So, you are called Meg and you live at The Dead Duck.'

She drew her knife – the one she used for cutting purses. 'What are you going to do?' she asked.

8 The cutpurse and the coffin

I grinned. 'Make a deal with you,' I said.

Inside The Dead Duck we all sat around the table. Me and my family, Meg and her dad. The two men shook hands.

'It's a fine idea,' the Landlord said.

My father nodded. 'We take our show on the road again. But this time, Meg calls us "cheats" and starts a riot. While the mob are crowding round us, Meg nips their purses. We meet up later and share the money.'

We shared the money from Meg's purses and it was enough to buy us a horse and cart.

A week later we were on the road and travelling all around Britain. It was a hard and dangerous life we lived for the next five years.

But it kept us going through the hard days of Henry VIII's reign. In time we made enough money to buy a tavern and give up our lives of trickery and theft … though Father still makes some money from mumchance games.

Now, some people may say that what we did was not honest. It was cheating.

When we were caught we were put in the stocks and whipped. If Meg had been caught she could have been hanged.

When fat King Henry VIII cheated he got away with it because he was king.

When Father stabbed me it was a game and no one was hurt.

When Henry sent sly-eyed Anne Boleyn and his fifth queen, little Catherine Howard, to be beheaded it was for real.

So who was the biggest cheat?

Even Will Somers knows the answer to that ... and he's a Fool!

Afterword: The terrible truth

The Thief, the Fool and the Big Fat King is a story based on real people and events.

In Tudor times, St Paul's churchyard in the centre of London was a meeting place for all sorts of people. Even in the church itself, traders bought and sold stuff. There were shows in the churchyard and some of them were tricks – made to fool people into giving money. The pig's bladder trick worked well, though one day a drunken 'victim' forgot to put a wooden board under his shirt and was really stabbed to death.

King Henry VIII took the throne when his father died and was one of the richest kings in the world.

But he wasted his careful father's wealth. His court fool was Will Somers, and we know a little about Will because several books were written about him.

By the time Henry married Anne Boleyn, he didn't have a lot of money to waste on card games. He'd spent it all. Henry loved to play – but hated to lose.

He was like a big spoilt child – he had to have his own way. When he didn't get it he turned violent and two of his wives were beheaded because of his vicious temper.

Henry VIII was not the sort of man you'd want to play cards with – or, if you did, you'd be happy to lose your money to save your life!

Look out for other
Tudor Tales
by bestselling author Terry Deary!

The Actor, the Rebel and the Wrinkled Queen

Elizabeth I is a mean queen –
with hands like claws, a wrinkled
white face and rotting teeth.
James Foxton is a young player
in Shakespeare's theatre company.
When the actors are caught
up in a rebellion, James finds himself
at the cold Queen's mercy …

The Maid, the Witch and the Cruel Queen

Everyone fears 'Bloody' Queen Mary who burns her enemies at the stake! Lord Scuggate gets ready for her visit by rounding up victims. But when he picks on the old wise woman, he finds he's made a big mistake …

The Prince, the Cook and the Cunning King

When a thin, pale boy called
Lambert claims he's the rightful
heir to the throne, King Henry VII
is furious! Mean King Henry has
clever ways of dealing with this
young impostor. Can Eleanor,
the maid, discover the truth –
and what will it mean
for Lambert?